An I Can Read

W9-BLQ-402

MICE AT BAT

story and pictures by
KELLY OECHSLI

HarperTrophy
A Division of HarperCollins*Publishers*

Mice at Bat
Copyright © 1986 by Kelly Oechsli
All rights reserved. No part of this book may be used or
reproduced in any manner whatsoever without written
permission except in the case of brief quotations
embodied in critical articles and reviews. Printed in the
United States of America. For information address
HarperCollins Children's Books, a division of
HarperCollins Publishers, 10 East 53rd Street,
New York, NY 10022.

Library of Congress Cataloging-in-Publication Data
Oechsli, Kelly.
    Mice at bat
    (An I can read book)
    Summary: When the human baseball game is over,
two teams of mice take over the ball park to play
their own championship ball game.
    [1. Baseball—Fiction. 2. Mice—Fiction] I. Title.
II. Series.
PZ7.027Mi 1986   [E]   85-45266
ISBN 0-06-024623-5
ISBN 0-06-024624-3 (lib. bdg.)
ISBN 0-06-444139-3 (pbk.)

First Harper Trophy edition, 1990.

To Helen,

who calls them as she sees them

Kevin and his friends
lived in a baseball park.
Every night they watched the game,
and they waited.
When the game was over,
the fans went home.

Then the lights went out,

and Kevin yelled,

"Okay, Mighty Mites!

It is cleanup time!"

Popcorn!

Peanuts!

Hot dogs!

They always found surprises.

"Okay!" Kevin shouted,

"We picked up all the food

Now it is practice time.

Jog around the bases!

Deep knee bends in left field!

Push-ups in right field!

Running and sliding at home plate!

Pitchers, follow me!"

Rusty's fastball sizzled.

José caught everything.

Young Willie broke only two bats.

And no one tripped over first base.

"We are looking good, Mites!"

cried Kevin.

The Mighty Mites were busy

batting and running,

sliding and yelling.

No one saw

Old Casey the cat

creep onto the field.

"Run!" shouted Lou.

"It is that pest, Old Casey.

He ruins everything."

"Hold it, everyone!"

Old Casey shouted.

"I have a letter for you."

Kevin took the letter
and read it out loud.

15

We challenge the Mighty Mites

to the Big Game—

Saturday at midnight.

Sharp!

signed...*The Boomers*

"Hurray!" cheered the Mighty Mites.

"The Big Game at last!"

Old Casey was not cheering.

Kevin thought he knew why.

"Casey, you know baseball.

Will you be the umpire?"

"Who, me?" said Old Casey.

"Yes! Yes!" shouted the Mighty Mites.

"Old Casey for ump!"

"Okay," said Old Casey. "Thanks."

Now he was smiling.

"All right, Mighty Mites!" said Kevin.

"Let us show those Boomers

we play the best ball in town."

Every night

the Mighty Mites batted

and ran

and slid

and planned for the Big Game.

Lou called the newspapers

and the radio stations.

Posters were put up.

At last the big night came.

"This is it, team," said Kevin.

"We will meet

in front of the Boomers' ball park.

Be there at midnight. Sharp!

Get there any way you can.

Good luck!"

Some went by subway.

Some went by tugboat.

Some just went.

At midnight

Kevin took the roll call.

All the Mighty Mites were there.

The air was cool.

The moon was full and bright.

It was a great night for a ball game.

The Mighty Mites ran onto the field.

"Hurray!" shouted the fans.

The Boomers ran onto the field.

"HURRAY!" shouted the fans.

Old Casey met with the two captains.

"Everybody plays," he said.

"And nobody argues."

"Shake," said Kevin.

"Shake," said Artie.

"PLAY BALL!" called Old Casey.

Young Willie stepped up to the plate.

The Boomers' pitcher wound up.

He threw the first pitch—

CRACK!

Willie hit the ball.

It flew

over the second baseman's head.

Lou was up next—*CRACK!*

The ball flew over the fence.

When their turn at bat ended,

the Mighty Mites had three runs.

Then the Boomers came to bat.

CRACK! CRACK! CRACK! CRACK!

They scored four runs.

The fans went wild.

"This is some game,"

said one fan.

"This is the game of the year!"

cried another.

In the second inning,

the Mites played better.

Young Willie threw the ball.

José caught it.

"Out! Out!" shouted Old Casey.

Each inning the Netter

caught everything in sight.

But the Boomers stayed ahead

4 to 3.

In the seventh inning

the Mighty Mites took the lead.

They scored five runs.

Then the Boomers were up.

CRACK! CRACK! CRACK!

They loaded the bases.

"TIME OUT!" called Artie.

"I am calling in Big Jax."

"Who is Big Jax?" asked Kevin.

Artie smiled.

"He is our pinch hitter."

Big Jax marched to the plate.

The Mites ran to the umpire.

"He is not one of us!"

the Mites yelled.

"But he *is* one of us," said Artie.

"He is wearing our uniform."

"I smell a rat,"

muttered Young Willie.

40

Old Casey looked in the rule book.

Then he shook his head.

"RAT. . .er. . .BATTER UP!"

he called.

Big Jax waved the bat

high over his head.

"Watch out, mister pitcher,"

he called.

"If you throw that ball

near the plate,

I will blast it to the moon."

Rusty pitched a fastball

right over the plate.

CRACK-K-K!

Big Jax was not kidding.

He hit that ball

right out of the park.

The score was tied.

Soon the Boomers were ahead
by eight runs.

Big Jax came to bat a second time.

CRACK!

Big Jax showed Young Willie
his way of sliding
into home plate.

"TIME OUT!" called Kevin.

"Are you all right?"

he asked Young Willie.

"Sure," said Young Willie.

"Let's get those runs back!"

"PLAY BALL!" yelled Old Casey.

As the sky got lighter,

The Mighty Mites' chances

got dimmer.

The Boomers were ahead 25 to 14.

The Mites were down

to their last out.

The Boomers put the Great Zipper

in to pitch.

ZING went the Great Zipper's ball.

CRUNCH went Young Willie's bat.

Now the count was two balls

and two strikes

and no bats.

"Bring out

a big one!"

yelled Kevin.

It took twelve Mites

to roll out the big bat.

"Where is the strike zone?"

asked the Great Zipper.

"Over the plate," said Old Casey.

"You pitch them, I call them."

The Great Zipper pitched.

"Everybody get ready!

Swing!" yelled Kevin.

"Wait! Not this one!"

shouted Lou.

"It's too fast!"

It was too close, too.

"BALL THREE," called the umpire.

The next pitch hit José's tail.

"HIT BATTER! TAKE YOUR BASE!"

The twelve Mites

trotted down to first.

Rusty was up next.

"I cannot lift that big bat,"

said Rusty.

He found a scorecard pencil.

"Now I am ready!" he yelled.

"Okay, Mites," said Kevin,

"there are two outs.

When Rusty hits the ball,

take off and keep running!"

Rusty hit a hard ground ball.

The twelve Mites

took off from first base.

The Boomers could not see

where the ball went.

The Mites passed second base,

then third.

They were heading for home!

Big Jax found the ball.

He threw it to home plate...

but the Mighty Mites

got there first!

Twelve times the umpire called,

"SAFE!"

Twelve runs were in.

The Mighty Mites were ahead 26 to 25.

When the Boomers came to bat,

they had no luck with Big Jax,

or the big bat,

or the pencil.

After three easy outs

the game was over.

The fans cheered.

It was a great night

for the Mighty Mites.

Even the Boomers said so.

"We will meet again next year
at your ball park," said Artie.
"And we will remember to bring
plenty of bats."

The happy Mites headed for home

any way they could.

Some went by subway.

Some went by tugboat.

Some just went.

63

It was time for a good day's sleep.

And dreams

about the night games to come.